For Asha and Hannah
and all the mothers and fathers
who only ever get to 2⅞

Published in 1991 by Magi Publications,
in association with Star Books International, 55 Crowland Avenue, Hayes, Middx UB3 4JP

Printed and bound in Hong Kong
Produced by Mandarin Offset
© Text, Ewa Lipniacka, 1991
© Illustrations, Basia Bogdanowicz, 1991

ISBN 1 85430 195 0

To bed · · · OR ELSE!

Written by Ewa Lipniacka
Illustrated by Basia Bogdanowicz

Magi Publications, London

HANNAH!

Asha and Hannah were friends
and neighbours

– the best of friends,
and the best of neighbours.

They shared a birthday.
They shared their books.
They even shared their toys …

... most of the time.

Their mums were also friends and they shared, too – they shared their children. If Hannah's mum had to go out in the evening, Hannah stayed with Asha.

And if Asha's mum had to work late,

Asha moved in, with just a few of her things,
to stay at Hannah's.

But the more they were together,
the noisier they became.
And Hannah's mum just could not get them to bed.

She read them a story ...

and another ...

and another.

She sang songs till her throat was sore,

cast shadows on the wall till she was weak,

and still they would not sleep.

So then she got very cross. "That's it!" she thundered.
"By the time I count to three, you two are in bed, asleep,
dreaming the sweetest of sweet dreams ... OR ELSE!!!"

"OR ELSE – what?" asked Asha and Hannah, together.
"O-N-E!" yelled Hannah's mum,
and she even slammed the door behind her.
"What does your mummy do for OR ELSEs, Hannah?"

"She usually just shouts a lot," said Hannah.
"That's not bad enough for an OR ELSE," declared Asha,
"OR ELSEs are much, much worse than that."

"She might put us out for the dustmen."

"She could give away all your toys to a jumble sale.
That's a really mean OR ELSE."

"T-W-O!"

"She might never, ever buy us ice cream again …

… and give us horrible medicine instead."

"TWO-AND-A-HALF !"

"Hannah, can she do magic OR ELSEs?
Could she turn us into frogs?"

"TWO-AND-THREE-QUARTERS!"

"What if she baked us in a pie and ate us all up?"
"She wouldn't, would she?" said Hannah.
"She just might," fretted Asha, "and then I would
never see my mummy again."

"TWO-AND-SEVEN-EIGHTHS!"

"Hannah, I'm scared. I don't think I like OR ELSEs."
"Me neither."
"Let's go to sleep – very, very quickly."
"Yes, let's."

And believe it or not – they did.

"Peace at last," thought Hannah's mum,
as she cleared up the mess and tucked them in.
"Another lucky escape ..."

"I just don't know what I would have done
if they hadn't gone to sleep!"